Hungry
Floppy

Written by Roderick Hunt
Illustrated by Alex Brychta

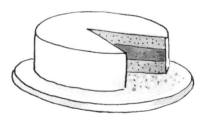

The family went camping. They
put up a tent.

It took a long time to put up the
tent. Floppy was hungry.

Floppy was so hungry, he ran
off to look for food.

A man was cooking.

"That smells good," thought Floppy,

"and I'm so hungry."

"Go away!" called the man.
"You can't have our dinner."
Floppy ran off.

Floppy saw a dog's bowl.
"This smells good," he thought,
"and I'm so hungry."

A big dog barked at Floppy.
"Go away," growled the dog.
"You can't have my dinner."

Floppy was lost. He saw lots
of tents but they all looked
the same to him.

Floppy could smell something.
He sniffed and sniffed. Something
smelled good.

Floppy went inside the tent.
He saw three plates. There was a
slice of cake on each one.

By now, Floppy was *very* hungry.
So he ate the big slice.

He was still hungry, so he ate the
smaller slice.

But Floppy was *still* hungry, so he ate the very small slice, too.

"I need a rest now," he thought.

There were three beds. Floppy lay on the blue bed, but it was too hard.

Then Floppy lay on the green
bed, but it was too soft.

In the end, he lay on the red bed.
It was not too hard or too soft. It
was just right. So he went to sleep.

Soon, a girl came back to the
tent with her mum and dad.
It was Anneena!

"Someone has eaten my cake,"
said Anneena.

"Someone has eaten *all* the cake,"
said Anneena's mum. "And look
who's sleeping on your bed."

"It's Floppy!" said Anneena. "What are you doing here, you naughty dog?"

Anneena and her dad looked
for Biff and Chip. At last, they
found them.

"What a surprise to see you!"
said Biff.

Anneena told them about Floppy.

"Never mind," said Dad. "Stay
and have some of our cake."

Talk about the story

Why did Floppy steal the food? Was he wrong to steal it?

Why didn't Floppy go and look for Biff and Chip himself?

How is this story like Goldilocks and the Three Bears?

What would you do if you got lost in a strange place?

Matching pairs

Find pairs of things that start with the same letter.
Which one isn't in the story?